T0022731

LOCUST HOUSE
A NOVELLA
HOUSE
ADAM GNADE

Three One G/Pioneers Press
PO Box 178262
San Diego, CA 92177-8262
www.pioneerspress.com
www.threeoneg.com

Cover and book design: Brandon Thomas McMinn
Edited by Jessie Duke
Cover photo credits: Shyann Weeks. Model Sarah Schmallen
Author photo credits: Elizabeth Thompson

ISBN: 978-1-939899-24-8

April 2016

"Adam Gnade's *Locust House* is a vast and eloquent document only he could tell. Full of life, loss, and a one of a kind 'beyond' that takes the reader through dimensions of humanity, sound, and vision encapsulated in a tiny window of time never to be repeated again. A testament to Southern California's glory days of recklessness, abandon, and blistering underground music, *Locust House* burned in my hands until the end with fresh, unbridled joy. A+" –Eric Wood of Bastard Noise

"*Locust House* is a love letter to a time: San Diego, the early 2000s, the moment in youth right before cynicism slips in. Like any true love letter, it accounts not just beauty and tenderness, but the dirty repercussions of love–the betrayals, the pain, the deaths." –Juliet Escoria, author of *Black Cloud* and the forthcoming *Witch Hunt*

"*Locust House* reads like James Joyce and E. Annie Proulx had a lovechild and dropped him into the punk scene of early '00s San Diego, and then 15 years later he wrote a novella. Adam Gnade has managed to pack more energy, story, and feeling into this novella than you will find in most full-length novels. It's as though he's written the literary equivalent of the 45-second songs he mentions in the book. It'll fuck you up like the best music, and like the best music, it'll haunt you long after you read the final sentence." –Jessie Lynn McMains, author of the forthcoming *What We Talk About When We Talk About Punk*, Poet Laureate of Racine, Wisconsin 2015-2017

"There's something so totally fucking intimate about a well-written book about incendiary events that the words just blow an IMAX experience away as a meaningless Hollywood effect. You're not just viewing from a distance–you're fucking in it, in it, in it. Adam recalls in one part the first time music did it for him, maaan, thanks for reminding me about how words can do it for me. Got lost in it, all of it!" –Martin Atkins of P.I.L., Ministry, Pigface

"*Locust House* makes me want to call up all of my teenage punk friends to ask if they ever still listen to those same CDs. *Locust House* confirms that I already know the answer. I feel nostalgic. I feel hopeful, I felt everything at once when I read the words, 'I wasn't cool but I was free.'" –Lucy K. Shaw, author of *The Motion,* co-editor of *the Shabby Dollhouse Reader*

"We work so hard at trying to exist, subconsciously looking at each other to find a cool belief to identify with. Survival without a solid foundation is brutal. I envy this particular S.D. crew coming together through the most extreme music/chaos—total excitement, totally identified. I really wish I'd gone to the Locust House with the Blood Brothers, I remember being invited to go. Man ..." –Ross Robinson, music producer for At the Drive-In, Head Wound City, The Cure

"*Locust House* eats the heart of Saturday Nite. Then worries that the meat was rancid, if it was meat at all? Forces itself to puke, and always fights for another taste. Adam grinds starry innocence against sinister abuses of trust, the tectonic shifting of once-close friends and other nicks of ordinary life shitty-ness to produce an honest work that shows what it loves and will make you feel, in a rare way, connected." –John-Vincent Greco author of *Torch Ballads* and *Death in a Rifle Garden*

"Blink and it's over. Hits like a plague of locusts. Windmilling unabashedly between the extremes of confidence, spiraling doubt, blood, fire, loneliness, siblinghood, and self-righteousness; grandiose and earnest but too cool to be in the room and desperate to belong to something better at the same time. Wait, was I supposed to be talking about the bands or the book?" –Julia Eff, author of *Every Thug is a Lady: Adventures Without Gender*

"*Locust House* could only have been written by someone who lived firsthand the ethos of the San Diego punk movement, someone who sweated and bled in the house party basements. Adam Gnade writes with the kind of passion and empathy that most writers take decades to achieve. His writing is somehow both youthful and wise, funny and sad. He tells stories about San Diego with the kind of love and nuance that only a native could have. His writing will lift you up then punch you in the gut, and you'll thank him for it." –Bart Schaneman, author of *Someplace Else: On Wanderlust, Expatriate Life, and the Call of the Wild*

More books by Adam Gnade

Hymn California (DutchMoney Books, 2008)

California (Double Suns, Oxford, UK, 2010)

The Do-It-Yourself Guide to Fighting the Big Motherfuckin' Sad (Pioneers Press, 2013)

Caveworld: A Novel (Pioneers Press/Punch Drunk Press, 2013)

INTRODUCTION

We created a place between the moth and the web, a kind of landmark that was and still is indefinable. It's a parallel dimension of sorts. It was never really about the music, or the art, but more so about a means of communication. Dabbling in telepathy and weird subconscious activism, something was carved in time and space. Even the time signatures and the timbre of sounds can be whatever we want them to be, if we put forth some sort of effort. Maybe it will make sense when we physically leave this planet, but for now, we can attempt to reflect on something we had all been part of, and try to grow and even evolve from it. Adam tells a story of a time in history that is relevant and worthy of passing on as we look for the next step in our concept of what existence means to us. It's the true essence of punk ethics. It's simplicity and complexity and everything in between wrapped into one brief moment in time. It's survival to grasp at humanity constantly slipping, all in hopes to un-fuck the world without even knowing what we were doing. For this, I thank Adam.

Justin Pearson
November 27, 2015

San Diego, California, 2002

Chapter 1
The Adventures of Agnes McCanty

Looking back, Agnes McCanty would come to see March 29th, 2002 as a day broken into three stages:

1) Standing at the gravesite of Michael the Bear.

2) A view of the sea from atop the rollercoaster then sex with Steven Boone in the backroom of the Halloween store.

3) The final night on E Street and how much she bled and how she felt like an arm held out a speeding car window.

The first: Standing at the gravesite of Michael the Bear in Sherman Heights—his bronze and black Keller-Holland casket like a train car, eye-level for a girl of five foot one, blocking out the sun which glared around it, golden but soft, dusk coming.

Agnes thought of the man who lay inside. Michael the Bear, her father's uncle, an Irishman (raised in England), though 40 years in the States (Pacific Grove [10 years], Watsonville [12], then San Diego [18]). Before that a pub cook in Coventry (two years) then an RAF pilot in the Second World War (26 months). Michael the Bear, the man who cared for Agnes after her mother passed away (breast cancer) and her father went to jail (for his brother-in-law's murder).

Michael the Bear stepped in, selfless, noble, loyal to Agnes—

3

forever loyal, his defining characteristic. What else? He was strong but wouldn't stoop to violence (which he told Agnes was unbecoming, as was backbiting, complaining, self-pity, selfishness). He was classy, she decided, yes, whatever classy meant he was that. This had nothing to do with money, which he had, but rather an overriding trait of his upbringing, his generation, and his content of character.

Michael the Bear was a man who liked people, who quietly loved anyone fighting to do a good thing—whatever it was, the goal mattered less than the path there. The final objective itself was unimportant, or secondary.

Agnes stood at the gravesite next to her cousins (who smelled like cigarettes and shampoo) and thought of his face—dark, dignified, high forehead, crow's feet around the eyes, hair swept back in a mane like a lion's, a voice like Liam Neeson's, deep and slow and resonate with bass—a calm voice, husky on the "w"s and soft vowels, telling her she was a good woman, that she had grown up well, that he missed her around the house but understood her absence.

The day he died Agnes found the body.

The door was locked but she had a key and she stopped in on the way to band practice the day the wildfires swept over East County.

The night before she had dreamt of skulls of sheep washing up on the beach—though huge, whale-size, rolling in the surf.

It was a dry day and it was hot and you could smell smoke and ash in the air from the blaze. Somewhere down the street a dog barked—yipped—as she unlocked the front door.

Agnes heard the sound of the breeze in the eucalyptus.

She pulled the door shut behind her.

The front room was quiet and still and there were dust motes moving in the light of the side-yard window.

She called his name.

The mouth of the hallway was dark—a black rectangle, open, featureless. She stepped into it and called out to him again as she walked down the hall.

4

In the bedroom Michael the Bear was under the big denim quilt. He ... no, not he, she thought, his *body, it,* not *he,* was facing the wall. A giant, six foot four even at his age, a flattened mountain or a cinder cone, motionless. His body was still in a way that the living never are.

The room was cold.

She dropped to her knees.

Michael the Bear was 82 and it was "coming" (her cousin Mary Lynn said on the car ride to the cemetery) but it would never happen today, some other day perhaps, not today, today would be fine, he would be here today. Anyway, why say goodbye to the living? Why sum up your time with someone when their time has not come?

"Hummingbird" was his name for her. Riding on his big shoulders at the Del Mar Fair, age four, talking in her high, piping voice, tiny hands too tight around his neck, but he didn't mind. He loved her with a burning pride, a strong, tremendous, substantial love; she couldn't hurt him. No one could. He was a stone, a castle wall, a locked drawbridge but a drawbridge that would open if she (or anyone worthwhile) asked. He was tough without being hard and that was the thing that made her feel safest.

Over the years Michael the Bear told Agnes some variation of the following in his slow, rolling, measured tone: "Hummingbird, if you can grow up tough without becoming mean or bitter or sour or cynical you'll do just fine." He said things like, "Remember Hummingbird, life is about finding as much happiness as you can without hurting anyone in the process. You won't find the meaning of life (but you'll look, if you're any good, and I know you are). What you will find is truths like that. True ways to live. That is one of mine, and it can be yours as well. Enjoy life violently but never be violent. Violence is the tool of cowards."

Agnes loved Michael the Bear with a fierceness she would not begin to understand until she was a parent herself. It was the true, animal fierceness of a blind cub in a den, of the small protected by the

5

strong. Now that he was gone (gone entirely, and unavailable to her) nothing she could do would allow her to speak to him again, which is what she wanted more than anything. Less to say goodbye than to ask him where he was; she couldn't imagine him so far gone as to be nowhere, as to not exist. His body, that was nothing, where was *he*? Where was the big, honest, courageous, tireless spirit that was Michael the Bear? A good thing like that doesn't die.

" ... and now safe ... in heaven ... with *God*," said the preacher. He didn't know Michael the Bear. He was hired from St.-Matthew's-by-the-Sea. A hired man. "Martin Schrader," he called him. Who was Martin Schrader? *Michael Schroeder* was Michael the Bear. There is no Martin Schrader, no, not here, not lying in there. "Mr. Schrader ... a good man ... in God's providence ... after a long ... *fine* life." Droning, enjoying a long pause and the sound of his own voice, but disinterested in the meaning. Agnes smelled rum on his breath on the walk across the lawn.

The smell of the flowers was sickening. She wanted nothing more than to set fire to the pile of them and push the preacher down into the blaze. She wanted to burn him to cinders for giving Michael the Bear an improper send-off. Stomp on his skull 'til it smashed flat and his brains burst out like cold pork gravy. Pull his spine from his body and beat the ground with it. Beat the ground and mourn Michael the Bear. Mourn him with blood speckling her arms, misting the air.

Agnes felt like a monster. She wanted to scream. She wanted to let loose her rage until the whole world shook. Agnes couldn't be kind like Michael the Bear. Not now. She wanted violence. She wanted to *be* violence.

The next few hours are remembered in a gauzy flash of images.

They were as follows:

Cresting the hill of the Giant Dipper rollercoaster at Belmont Park with her cousins Daniella and Mary Lynn after the funeral. A redheaded boy her age sitting in the coaster car next to her who

6

smelled like old pasta floating in a pot of water. He held the metal bar in front of him and looked seasick as they rose up the track.

Earlier, on the car ride back from the cemetery, the green blur of Balboa Park flashing by:

"We have to kill an hour," said Mary Lynn, driving. She wore big sunglasses with white plastic frames and her dyed blonde hair moved around her face in the breeze.

Daniella leaned in from the backseat. Cigarette breathe. "Hotbox Yoda the Toyota and ride the rollercoaster?"

"*Hells* yeah. Let's do it. Agnes?"

"Huh?"

"Agnes, you wanna get stoned and ride the Dipper?"

"It doesn't matter."

And it didn't.

Or did it?

She sat in the beach parking lot while her cousins laughed and passed the pipe from the front-seat to the back.

Did it matter?

What mattered?

It didn't matter.

Then: after the clacking assent up the rollercoaster track and before the plunge downwards, there was a view of the sea—silvery and wind-chopped, cold, vast, rolling with long lines of swell.

It never ends, thought Agnes.

Next: the drop down and her hair blowing straight back and the tightening of her stomach muscles as her cousins screamed happily, arms held up. They took the turn hard, the wheels rattling, jostling on the track, the wind in her face, gritting her jaw, strained, nauseous.

Next: ditching her cousins at the amusement park in the dark of the arcade, Agnes walked down Mission Boulevard alone with the evening traffic all around and the wind whipping her hair into her eyes. Storefronts, surf shops, beach bars, grains of sand under her shoes on

7

the sidewalk, traffic lights in the dusk.

Next: asking her boyfriend Steven for a ride home at his uncle Carl's Halloween store.

"I'm sorry to ask but—"

"No, it's cool, that works. Come back here a sec."

"Here?"

"Just c'mon."

Steven took her hand and they walked past the walls of masks—ghoulish faces, hairy, mouths open, cut-out holes for eyes, screaming silently, devil beards, worms and maggots nestling in wounds, bloody teeth, fanged, rubbery, howling without sound, horrible mouths—and into the back room while Big Marcos the new hire sat at the register reading a comic book. There was gray light (a fading light) through the windows, and Big Marcos, frowning down at the book, turning the pages with a soft, fat hand as Spider-Man swung through the city after the Green Goblin, casting his webs left and right.

Next: in the back room, Steven, shoving her forward against the counting desk on her belly, her skirt pulled up to her waist, her panties to her ankles, and pushing up inside her, before she was ready.

"Slower," she said. "Ow, Steven. Slow *down*."

"I'm ... trying."

"Take your ... time. Slower. Steven! Not yet. No ..."

It was over fast. One hand on her waist, gripping, his nails digging into her flesh, the other clawing her right breast until it hurt, his hips smacking against her, and he came into Agnes "like a dish soap bottle squeezed into a tub of warm water," he told Big Marcos with a laugh while Agnes cleaned up in the bathroom. "Agnes, she's a mess but she's a hot little fuck," he said. "Check it, take my keys. Drive her home. If you want to fuck her you totally can. I bet she'd at least suck your dick. My brother Ted's in town. The three of us should get her drunk and try to run a train on that little bitch." (Big Marcos, overwhelmed and upset by the proposition, took a smoke

8

break before driving Agnes home. The next day he would quit Steven's uncle's Halloween store and apply [unsuccessfully] at the Clairemont Party City before landing his dream job at the Karl Strauss Brewery by the freeway. Eight years later he would add Steven on Facebook and send him the following message: "Dude, that shit you said about your girlfriend and us having sex with her? That was so not okay. I've been thinking about that for years and I had to get it out. That was a shitty, evil thing to say." The message received no reply and Big Marcos was promptly unfriended.)

On the drive back to Golden Hill, Big Marcos hummed along with the car stereo while Agnes sat in the passenger seat and felt small and used-up and unimportant. To clear her mind, she thought of Michael the Bear's favorite things to cook:

1) Once a week: lasagna with Italian sausage. Later, as a substitution, butternut squash ravioli with brown butter, sage, and shaved parmesan when she quit eating meat. For both: side of garlic bread. A spinach and cabbage salad with halved red grapes, kalamata olives, marinated artichoke hearts, and goat cheese (later, baked tofu).

2) On the rare chilly nights in the winter they would sit around the small kitchen table and eat thick split pea soup cooked with carrots and bacon (and, later, liquid smoke or Bacos). On the side: sourdough bread. The serving of the bread: butter and a squeeze of lemon, a result of Michael the Bear's four years working at Bozic's (1976-1980), a seafood restaurant on Clairemont Mesa Boulevard.

3) On summer days when it was too hot to move he made gazpacho with a pitcher of strawberry lemonade. For dessert: peach ice cream garnished with a sprig of mint. Michael the Bear maintained what he called a "Victory Garden," and with San Diego's long growing season a good portion of each meal came from what he grew. She saw him standing at the kitchen counter of the old North Park house, slicing

9

lemons in the late-afternoon light, saying, "Agnes, everyone must know how to grow their own food. When you cut yourself off from that you shut the door on something older than history, something important and deep to our character."

Agnes thought of his meals and his happiness (and how serious he was) as he prepared them.

She stared out the window at the growing dark, the sunset behind the car like a wall of fire consuming the Earth.

Don't fucking cry, she told herself. *Not in front of him.*

Stopped at a traffic light across from the Nuevo Cristo church she saw a wedding party push open the big doors and come out from the gold-lit square of the hall and down the steps, the bride in front, holding up her dress to walk.

She imagined Michael the Bear giving her away at her own wedding. How proud he would be (and how stirred his big heart) as he answered the words, "Who gives this woman away?"

"That would be me."

It was night now and the bride's gown was so white it was nearly blue, like snow glowing against her dark skin and all the black suits and dresses and gray stone around her.

They made a left at the light.

"Isn't it kind of late in the day for a wedding?" she asked Big Marcos, who drove with one hand on the wheel, the other on his right thigh, tapping along to the radio.

He shrugged. He didn't know.

The singer on the radio was singing that if he could find that Heina and that Sancho that she's found, he would pop a cap in Sancho and smack her down, and Agnes wanted to die. For the first time in her life she wanted to die.

Big Marcos dropped Agnes off at her studio apartment in Golden Hill which sat between two Victorians in the shade of a grapefruit tree, a street lined with cars, the yellow lighted windows

10

blinking on in the darkness.

Walking up the brick path under the trees she heard *mariachi* music from the line of pink apartments across the street—fuzzy, barely there. She could smell onions and garlic frying in butter and a voice was yelling something distant, then laughter followed by frantic noise on TV, the war, or a riot.

Sleepwalking she opened the door, shut it behind her, and dropped her keys on the carpet. She stepped across the bare twin-size mattress on the floor and over her guitar and 4-track machine and a pile of tapes and cables as she pulled off her clothes, then three steps to the tiny bathroom.

The person in the mirror: pale skin, freckles across her nose, soft brown hair swept over her forehead and tucked behind her left ear, longer on the sides than the back, falling into pin-curls around her chin. The face was unsmiling and had empty slate-gray eyes.

She was wrung out, she decided, wrung out and so much older than 22. She ran her hands across her bare shoulders, a new mole on the rise of her collarbone, the tattoo of a one-winged locust on her chest above her left breast.

Agnes cupped her breasts in her hands and looked down at them, her bright pink nipples poking out from between her fingers. She shook her head. She saw the bathmat below her feet, orange, new but starting to wear. Steven's cum was dried on the inside of her right thigh. Her toenails were painted baby blue. She knew she was pregnant. Somehow she knew. She thought of his cock inside her and the sour smell of his body and her stomach went tight again as it had on the rollercoaster.

Bending down to turn the cold water knob, then the hot—hot to burn her flesh until she was able to forget.

In middle school she was called "the Pale Whale."

"It was before I lost my baby fat," she told her coworker Melanie Crenshaw fourteen years later near the dead-center of the country (Overland Park, Kansas) while they sat in the living room of

11

Melanie's new white townhouse drinking chardonnay with a plate of untouched Ritz crackers and sweet pickles.

"You were *fat?* I don't believe that."

"I wasn't fat ... I was ... I was a *kid.* It was the only time in my life I had tits but I looked awful. In high school my first boyfriend Travis Broadus called me 'the Pale Princess.' He meant it as a compliment but ... *ugh* ... I *hated* it. I hated being the Pale Princess even worse than the Pale Whale. That's why I called the band Pale of Shit."

"*What, Agnes!* Oh my god, girl. I didn't know you played music. Was it any *good?* I can't imagine you in a *band.* Agnes the little secretary in a band, like *what?*"

"It doesn't matter."

"What did it sound like?"

"It doesn't matter."

"*Come on.*"

"It's dumb. It ... it was a hardcore band. I played guitar and sa ... screamed. I screamed and played guitar. It was so dumb."

"Hardcore? Is that like—"

"Punk."

"Get *out.* No way. You were so not in a punk band."

"I was. Yeah, Pale of Shit," raising her hands above her head and shaking them, "Woo hoo." Laughing. Then not. "It was during college. I had my own apartment. A car that never ran. Yeah, a band. I was in a band. I was 22 and we broke up when I was ... god, like, 23, a year later maybe?"

"Wow, Ags, I can't imagine you like that. What *happened?*"

"Life? Growing up? I don't know."

"Do you still listen to that kind of music?" Sipping her wine. "If you can call it that."

"No, not at all," she said, lying. "I'm not that kid anymore."

The shower steamed the glass until Agnes was an outline in the mirror.

12

She stepped into the stall and pulled the curtain closed, the plastic rings clacking.

Agnes shut her eyes and let the water hit the back of her head and run down her shoulders.

Chapter 2
Golden Hill

As you move eastward from Agnes McCanty's studio apartment, which sits on the crest of the hill and on the far west edge of the neighborhood, the streets are wide and well-paved and lined with cars. It's an older part of town, or rather it feels older in contrast to Downtown with its expensive wine bars and dance clubs or the coastal area's beach resort sprawl. The houses in Golden Hill are (by in large) ratty but as lovingly well-maintained as a low to modest income will allow.

Driving up Broadway as the numbered streets rise, you will see Craftsman cottages, Victorians, turn-of-the-century bungalows, white stucco apartments in the California Motel style, crumbling Alpine facades, railroad apartments with French ironwork gates.

Inside the Victorians and Craftsmans are hardwood floors (in varying states of repair) and old glass cabinets and big windows (and window seats) with a view (facing west) of Downtown and the airport and shipyard, or (to the north, east, and south) rolling hills of tar shingle and orange tile rooftops.

The skies are blue and cloudless and the rain comes infrequently as with most deserts. And that is what San Diego is—a desert, but a desert in disguise, made green with the water of other (poorer) cities.

In the years since, the drought has come and the beautiful lawns are gone but a well-located coastal town will change in other ways. Development rolls in with tourist money (or the promise of it).

15

The San Diego of now is not the San Diego of then, just like the San Diego of then is not the San Diego of decades back, when the sleepy beach neighborhoods were closer to a post-War America.

Before that, it was ranchland and marsh flats and endless dirt fields of low scrub brush. Before that, the Spanish priests and the Mission above Old Town, and further back, native people—Luiseño, Cahuilla, Cupeño, Diegueño—small tribes in the arid, sun-baked, manzanita hills and bramble-land or (to the west) coastal villages with fish and pelts drying on wood racks, small fires, men and women pulling abalone from the tidepools. It was a quiet time when the loudest sound was the wind, which came (and comes) mostly from the west over the sea, an onshore wind, colder than the warm offshores (from the east) that blow over the deserts and spark brushfires in the drier rural parts of the county.

On March 29th, 2002 Golden Hill is a quiet part of town (in a different way than in the time of the Luiseños) and the development that's now spread across the county has yet to change the face of the neighborhood. Here (now, March, 2002) the predominant language is Spanish and muscle cars or hotrods sit in dusty driveways next to rabbit hutches or stacks of tires in the weeds or small gardens.

In the evening *mariachi* bands play backyard parties or birthdays or *quinceañeras*, with laughing families and candles lit on garden walls and strings of light over picnic tables. Window signs in Spanish announce sales on pork shoulders, tripe, cantaloupe. The neighborhood is full of taco shops, *mercados* and *carnicerías*, stately churches in the mission style or semi-gothic. In the middle of town is a laundromat with a sleeping cat in the window, and there are well-kept liquor stores and bars, shops selling US-to-Mexico phone cards and *piñatas* and sturdy cowboy boots. The trees are mostly palm trees and they line the hilly streets like telephone poles.

As you reach the eastern edge of town there are empty lots with dog shit dried white and old car batteries and the bones of cats and birds in the ice-plant and grass. There are abandoned apartments,

16

punk squats with kids outside drinking 40s, watching you drive past. There are condemned houses covered in graffiti, mostly names in elaborate, jagged shapes and colorful swirls or smiling cartoon animals or exaggerated taggers with huge heads and big sneakers and a can of Krylon spraypaint in hand. There are also political murals. Cesar Chavez in a sea of upturned faces. Martin Luther King with a finger raised defiantly next to his face. Che Guevara, stormy with his beard and beret. Or stencils of Mexican revolutionaries with rifles held above their heads and bandoliers of cartridges draped across their chests. Now these are gone, along with the muscle cars and rabbit hutches and empty lots. Now, in 2016, the young professionals who work in the Mission Valley and Downtown offices and the white college students have moved in and many of the Mexican families and most of the punks have moved south to Logan or Sherman Heights, or further still to Chula Vista or San Ysidro. But for now it's a quieter time. At night you can hear the sound of the freeway as you walk down Broadway and there are neons humming from storefronts and you can imagine yourself in 1950s America. Walking down C Street or 26th at dusk you will smell dinner cooking—*albóndigas, menudo, pozolé*, pots of beans (well-peppered), *chorizo, sopes* frying in oil.

James Jackson Bozic, 26, and Frances Alicio, 21, walk past the shopfronts and awnings lining 25th Street. It's night but most of the stores are still open.

They wait for traffic to clear then cross the street, passing the fruit stand (closed) and the laundromat (open), the smell of pineapples and dryer sheets in the air.

Frances hums to herself, the tune indistinct. They walk arm in arm and James thinks of his grandfather's .22 pistol in the sock drawer and the dusty light through the window as he slides the drawer open to look at it, on his tip-toes, six years old, La Veta, Colorado.

Frances thinks of dark trees in Georgia and sky behind them. She thinks of the footbridge over the stream in Hinesville and ring snakes bending through the grass and a crack of lightning running in

17

jagged crags across the sky.

Eugenio Armendáriz, 43, sells grilled corn from a stand on 25th. He wears a white t-shirt with a front pocket, light blue work pants, and black boots. As James and Frances approach he's thumbing through a copy of *The Reader.* He folds it under his arm and smiles and nods hello. He sees Frances and thinks of his daughter back in Mexico, standing at the water spigot, thin-armed, pale, struggling to fill a bucket for the goats, the sky overhead blue and cloudless, the musky smell of the creek in the air.

"*¿Qué onda?*" says James.

Eugenio nods. "*¿Quieren elote?*"

"*Sí, gustariamos dos, por favor.*"

Eugenio asks James if he wants cheese. "*¿Con queso or sin? Tenemos cotija.*"

"Frankie, you want cheese, right?"

"Yeah, please," she says.

Eugenio nods and smiles at her and takes the first ear of corn off the grill and rolls it in an aluminum serving dish of melted butter then drizzles it in dry white cheese. Next, a squeeze of fresh lime and a shake of cayenne pepper. He thinks of TV static as the channels change and a dark living room with people sitting on a couch. His daughter standing in the hallway door, head leaned on her arm against the jamb, the light of the TV on her face. John Wayne is onscreen in military attire, standing in front of a tank, squinting, saying, "Well, ya gone and done it *this* time didn't you?" His daughter says that Americans aren't really like that and her brother says "Shh."

The traffic clears and the street darkens.

The neons of the Turf Club glow green against the gray and black, and the windows of the laundromat are bright-lit and cheery. A pregnant woman moves inside, pulling wet clothes from a washer and setting them aside in a wire basket.

Now traffic again. Moving past. Slow. Yellow-white headlights, dull red brakelights, flashing.

18

Frances wraps her arm in James', her head on his shoulder. All is good. For now. For now all is good.

Joey Carr, 24, turns the corner, walking past Panchita's Bakery and Jaycee's Market, smoking a cigarette, drinking tequila from a Dr. Pepper can, staggering but comfortable, singing to himself.

Frances nods up the street, "James, is that Joey *Carr*?"

"Huh. Yeah. He looks like *shit*."

Eugenio asks James if he and Frances want something to drink.

James shakes his head. *"No gracias."*

"Pues ... tres dólares."

James opens his wallet and takes out a ten. *"Chilo. Dos por el propino. ¿Hay cambio?"*

"Si. Gracias, mijo."

Joey catches sight of them and half jogs up to the stand and then he's out of breath, leaned forward, hands on his knees. "James ... Jackson ... Bozic and Frances Alicio, what are you two vampires up to?" Laughing, standing up straight again, bringing his cigarette to his mouth, sucking in. His nails are painted black (and chipped) and his hands are sun-burnt. His hair is dirty and he's wearing eyeliner and he smells like weed and sweat. His stained white t-shirt reads "Le Shok Le Shok Le Shok" in hot pink letters.

James smiles. "We're going to the E. Street House show. It's their moving-out party. They got evicted."

"You should come with," says Frances.

Eugenio hands Frances a paper bag with the aluminum foil wrapped corn cobs inside. It's heavy. She can feel the heat through the bag and she can smell the butter and cayenne pepper.

"Thanks," she says.

"Thank you, *mijita*." He stares at her sadly and decides to call this daughter in the morning. In his mind he says he's sorry, *"Lo siento, Leti. Lo siento, mijita."*

Joey takes a drag and turns his head and blows the smoke

19

to the side. "Dude, no way, the Avocado Club's closing up shop? Bummers."

James nods. "Avocado Club? Who calls it that?"

"Some people do."

"I always just called it the Locust House," says Frances.

Joey's distracted. He looks across the street at the 7-11. "Yeah ... but like ... but like nobody else does." He looks back at James and Frances and smiles. His teeth are gapped and yellow. "I've always called it the E Street House but it's funny to say the Avocado Club because I'm all, No way, that shit's a *sandwich*, yo, not a house. You can't live in a sandwich!" He laughs and coughs. "That's shit's a ... it's a *sandwich*. Right?"

James shrugs. "I guess. I don't know. Anyway, it should be pretty fun."

"Who's playing?"

"Locust, Blood Brothers ... "

Joey flicks his cigarette into the street. "Sick."

James looks at the cigarette lying in the street, smoke still trailing up from it, moving with the breeze. A car passes over it and then he sees it again, the smoke still rising. "I think ... I think the new band with Omar and Cedric from At the Drive-In."

They step to the side so a woman with a toddler girl next to her can order.

"Necesito nueve," the woman tells Eugenio. " *Y tres* Pepsis."

Eugenio begins to work.

Joey pulls another cigarette from his pack. "At the Drive-In. No way, really? Is it Mars Volta?"

"No, I think it's called De Facto. Frankie, who else is playing?" James looks at Frances, shrugging, "Moving Units?"

Frances shakes her head. "Maybe? I don't know. But ... we should head out. James, you wanna do this? Yeah?"

"Yeah yeah yeah," says James. "Let's do it."

Joey lights the cigarette and sticks his lighter into his back pocket. "I'll see ya around maybe. I'm supposed to meet Curt at Reyes. We're goin' to I.B. to buy—" talking quieter now "—we're buying some shit to take down to Ensenada ... to sell ... if ... if you all want some."

James shakes his head. "Naw, that's cool."

"No thanks," says Frances.

"Alright, lates. See you two around. Don't go chasin' waterfalls." Joey laughs, then coughs again, holding his fist to his mouth. "Don't go chasin' waterfalls," he says again, hoping James or Frances will continue the line.

They don't.

"See ya," says James.

"Bye, Joey," says Frances.

James and Frances walk down 25th, Frances holding the bag of corn cobs under her right arm.

"Yeah, *that* was awful," James says. "What the fuck."

"Poor Joey. He's such a nice kid. I wish we didn't see that. What's he getting from Curt?"

"I don't know, heroin? Ugh, jeez. No good. No, no, no good. I fuckin' hate that guy Curt. His sister Elsa was cool. Sad about that, huh?"

"James, he looked like he was *eighty*."

"Yeah ... yeah, but we're going to the party and it'll be great."

"It will, right?"

"It will. Frankie, it will. It'll be great and who cares."

"Right, who cares. Agh, James but still ... still ... I feel like we just saw a *ghost*."

They stand at the stoplight.

Across the street on Broadway, Joey Carr drops his Dr. Pepper can in the trash and walks into the 7-Eleven.

Frances sees Tyler Monahan's dark blue Miata pull up to the curb and park on Broadway.

Tyler gets out, shuts his door, and waves at them emphatically.

21

"Hey guys!" he shouts from across the street. They don't hear it but they see him.

"James, look, Tyler."

"Nice. Hey, Tyler! Hey!"

Frances looks up as the light turns to green. Above them the black sky is streaked gray like lines of old scars on skin.

She thinks of relief maps, train tracks, dirty canals, Neosporin, hydrogen peroxide.

They cross the street.

24

Chapter 3
Battles and Aftermath

JAMES:

Frankie, Tyler, and I sat on a curb down by the overpass bridge and ate our corn and sipped Tyler's flask of rum. The rum felt warm in my belly and made my head swim nicely and the corn was damn good but Frankie and I could barely sit still. We wanted to go to the party. We wanted to see the bands. After we finished the corn we stopped at 7-Eleven for provisions and walked to the party. The place was packed by the time we got there. It was a very dark night. Foggy too, which is something that stands out in all my memories of Golden Hill. Foggy nights. Slow fog when it's so dark and there's no moon and that thick, beautiful mist creeps up from the canyons and freeways and the air is wet and smells like honeysuckle and night-blooming jasmine.

At the house a million kids were out smoking and drinking on the porch, a whole sea of them, and more than that on the lawn—sitting along the white picket fence that lined the sidewalk, lying in the grass with bottles and cigarettes in hand, or up on the rooftops of cars, coming in and out of the house, every square foot of the place was moving like it was covered in ants and you could hear music from inside, muffled but heavy, rumbling.

The street was lined with vans that the bands had come in and some of them had their side doors open and you could see all your heroes drinking or smoking or talking or just chilling before their set.

We walked past one of the bands standing outside their van on the sidewalk and I stopped the singer and I was like, "Hey, my name's

James. I'm a friend of your cousin Meggy. You guys's new record is so fucking good. I've listened to it like 200 times this week," and he kind of just shrugged and smiled and walked off.

I was young—younger than I am now—and very star-struck and nervous and so much more innocent than the person I've become, who I worry has a hard time feeling his blood some days.

As nerdy and uncool and on the outside of things as I was at the time, my move toward the opposite of that has come with a price. I won't say I'm jaded but I've never felt as thrilled by music, by white-hot, cranked, wild-eyed MUSIC, as I did back then. My love for good music was almost religious, or maybe sexual; it was pious, desperate. Good music made me feel hot-headed and frantic and I don't know if I've ever felt so free since. I wasn't cool but I was free and that was something good.

Frankie and Tyler and I walked up the sidewalk and we were so happy and so innocent and I was taking sips off this bottle of MadDog 20/20 orange flavor I got at 7-Eleven and was getting solidly drunk and it felt as though everything was new and alive and more colorful and vibrant than everyday life.

At the time I had a job as a reporter for a small wire service in Hillcrest and Frankie worked as an endoscopy clinic receptionist up in La Jolla. Our lives weren't bad but the nine to five sucked it out of us. It made us feel slow inside, muted, dead on our feet. It felt like we were wasting our time, but when we listened to these bands we loved, life seemed vital and strange and triumphant and real. What I'm trying to say is I had no arrogance, no stuffiness, no true or defined ego; I was terrified of living half the time and scared as hell of dying the rest. A lot of us were that way and we wanted nothing more than to sign off on real, hard, stupid life and listen to records that were like trains crashing into each other and dance clubs exploding into rainbows and carnivorous flowers devouring crickets at 10 times the normal speed.

We wanted punk rock but our version of punk didn't sound

26

like a band. It wasn't two guitars, bass, singer, drums. We wanted a sound that tore itself to pieces but did it SMART. We wanted grindcore turned inside out and sped up and then chopped to pieces by a machete the size of the universe. We wanted power violence with a big, loving heart and good ethics to match. We wanted punk you could DANCE to and never feel awkward or uncool or out of place. If anything I wanted to dance. I wanted to lose my mind and throw myself into walls and get sweaty and stupid and feel the raw animalness in me. I had many nights alone in our cottage in Golden Hill, sad-drunk after a bad day at work or a fight with Frankie, in the dark, dancing by myself in front of the record player, one hand on the bookcase. I needed bands like Angel Hair, Antioch Arrow, Get Hustle, Die Princess Die, Melt-Banana, Orchid, Black Dice, VSS, Man is the Bastard, Universal Order of Armageddon, Celebration. The best and the darkest, the wildest hearts.

I still remember the first time music really did it for me. It was at the Ché Café a couple years before the E Street party and the Locust came out of nowhere and imploded my world. Those short, abrupt, sinewy, 45-second songs wiped my brain clean, changed everything, scrambled my senses, showed me that music wasn't necessarily what everyone had told me it was.

Unlike a lot of people I've talked to I didn't have to work to "get" their music. It made sense immediately. Of course. Of course songs should be like this. Of course this is how music should be. That first song at the Ché was enough to change me for the better and the change was natural and easy and comfortable.

I didn't consider their music screamo or metal or anything else the critics called it; I began to see Locust songs as pop songs—danceable, rhythmic blasts of thrash and grime and humor and new, experimental ideas. A few months later Frances, Ben Frank, and I went to see the band open the premier of the John Waters film *Cecil B. Demented* at Hillcrest Landmark and they played the show in adult-size diapers—more or less naked in front of the big screen and

27

a sold-out crowd. Their set was about nine minutes long, and they played twice that many songs. Short, colorful, glittery, stutteringly abrasive, robotic seizure songs just as human as birth and life and sex and death.

After that we watched the movie, smiling like fools, slurping our sodas and picking at our popcorn and Junior Mints. In the scene that used their song "Nice Tranquil Thumb in Mouth" the characters show up at a Baltimore Film Commission luncheon and have a big shoot-out with the cops. "Thumb," my favorite song at the time, was looped to extend it and it was the catchiest thing in the world—toe-tapping, head-nodding but, oh man, so fucking savage and strange and brutal.

When the credits rolled and the band's name came up in the soundtrack list everyone cheered. I was proud. Proud of my city and the people in it and of this small moment in time. People were excited—excited and together about this thing. It was easy to get caught up in. Their music became a part of our culture. Not everyone's culture but for some of us it was as San Diego as the Tom's Deep Plate at Pokez and gothy wine-drunk dance-parties in North Park and talking shit about The Gaslamp.

There's this line from Cassavetes' great film *Opening Night* where Gena Rowlands' character says:

"When I was seventeen, I could do *anything*. It was so easy. My emotions were so close to the surface. I'm finding it harder and harder to stay in touch."

That's how it was. I mean, I wasn't exactly young. Frances was. I wasn't. But here's the thing, I was a ghost in high school. I had no friends to speak of and my everyday plan was survival. I wanted to live through the day without confrontation and get home so I could hide in my bedroom and what, I don't know, draw, read magazines, stare at the wall.

My youth was a total shit-storm. After elementary school, which was great, and so was my childhood—a good, ideal, sweet

28

one where I felt loved and safe and respected—I hit middle school like a piece of hamburger dropped on a grill. Walking the halls of P.B. Middle I felt like a fox hunted constantly in a world where no one had ever seen a fox but really, INTENSELY wanted to eat one on a bun with bacon and mayo. I hated bacon and I hated mayo but more than anything I hated myself. Of course, as it goes, people hated me because I hated myself and because of that I was scared of my shadow and inarticulate and full of heavy, awful, weapon's grade anxiety that sabotaged me at every step.

I wanted to die because I knew I was nothing and I wanted to die because I knew no one would ever care what I had to say. My life was powerless and I saw the future as a bland, stultifying thing that looked like those horrible shitheads from *Friends* sitting on a couch in some fancy-ass, well-lit, New York coffee shop trading mild insults. I hated them and I hated that the future—my future—was headed that way.

At the time I had no other frame of reference to tell me life could be something else. What I saw—what I *knew*—was what I was given by mainstream media and if adulthood looked like Must See TV I wanted out. No future. No fun. No hope. No beauty.

I was wrong of course but at that time—my true youth—I was a dog that had been kicked so often I flinched at every tremor.

I didn't have that impressionable, romantic, idealistic teenagehood like a lot of people. That came later. It came in my early twenties and it came when punk rock found me in the audience of that Ché show and dragged me in. It was a moment that arrived when I least expected it and beyond giving me good music it told me life could be shaped however you want as long as you work hard and dig for new options. The important thing was to fight every day to make your life what you wanted it to be. I had so many people telling me life had to be this one set thing and finding out I didn't have to listen to them—that I could come up with my own way to live—busted my world in two.

29

Which is to say I fell head over heals in love with the brutalist, smartest, meanest kind of punk rock and it opened up life like a giant window with all the sunlight in the world streaming in, and that all lead to the final house show at 2411 E Street.

The Avocado Club, the E Street House, the Locust House, whatever you called it the place was an epicenter for things free of bullshit, a burning, atomic centerpoint to the neighborhood and the scene and punk rock in general.

FRANCES:

One of my strongest memories of that time has less to do with the party than the aftermath. Everyone moved out of the house, right? and as soon as they were gone the new tenants hung an American flag from the second story.

It went suddenly from the cool house on the block where the best bands lived to the fucking White House. You have to remember this was just a year after 9/11 and a lot of us had some pretty, uh, I don't want to say, well, yeah, okay, anti-American sentiments at the time. We were angry and we felt let down. Some of us (a lot of us) were sure our government had caused it. Even if it wasn't an inside job like some people say, we were at the very least responsible for waging constant global war for money and calling it "justice."

It's an awful thing when you grow up thinking that you and your country are the good guys and then you find out it's all bullshit. The day I realized we weren't as noble as I'd been told ... fuck, man, it was a crushing moment. It changed me. I've never been the same.

From a very young age I've been looking for community. Most of the time you were let down but sometimes (if even for a short while) it felt like we were all in it together. That's how our scene felt and losing that house was a huge blow. Maybe not for everyone, maybe not even for the bands or the people who lived there, but for me it was a symbol of a better, smarter, more ethical life. It seemed firm and substantial; it felt like something that couldn't be taken away

30

from us.

That's one thing I've learned: People say there are things that can't be taken from you. Everything can be taken from you. The place you live, your friends, your family, your health, your youth, your sense of self or your dignity, your freedom, your confidence, your spirit, anything. There is nothing in you that's yours to keep if someone else wants it bad enough. You try to hold onto it but life is (inherently, unfairly) violent.

From our scene, and even more so at that last party, I felt a kind of togetherness that was like what we experienced in the weeks following 9/11. People were suddenly good to each other and it seemed like we were all closer than we were before. Of course that was over fast (in both circumstances). The party was shut down by the cops and everyone left. People stopped watching the news after the attacks because they couldn't take the footage. (Or because they had to live their lives, to get by, to keep moving. I understand that.)

I remember sitting on the couch at my mom's house with James and my sisters Sadie and Rebecca watching the news reports with the towers burning and people jumping out, holding hands, falling, falling, ugh, and us sitting there, crying all day, so scared, so *uncertain*. Around dinnertime a couple of my friends showed up with a fucking pizza. They wanted to hang out then go to a show at the Ché or the Epicentre or somewhere.

I was like, "What the *fuck*?" I didn't say "What the fuck?" but I did say, "Haven't you guys been watching the *news*?"

My friend Timmy Willits (standing in the doorway, holding the pizza box) shrugged and said, "Kind of. I know something happened but like—" but they didn't care.

People move on or they don't feel something as deeply as they should. I thought that after 9/11 there would be some kind of greater togetherness in our culture just like I felt as though the energy of that party would carry on. In both cases I was wrong and it was incredibly isolating. Situations like those are moments of innocence and once

31

innocence is replaced by cynicism (or even a lack of concern) it can deal a heavy blow. You experience closeness but then it's a temporary closeness and once you realize that it's over then things start feeling pretty lonely.

I've always wanted people to join together, in their neighborhoods, their scenes, or in their families, whatever it is, but the fact of the matter is Americans are bad at togetherness. We're afraid of it or we label it as this dangerous, subversive thing, this toxic kind of discord in the face of "rugged American individualism," which is nothing but bullshit and self-sabotage. Or we find it and it feels so good (it feels *natural*) but just as soon as we're brought together we either let go or allow ourselves to be pulled away from each other. Or we stop caring. We find other things to take up our interest. We get distracted.

I wanted to take the flag off that porch and burn it just like I wanted to kick George W. Bush's grave half-smirking monkey face in. I wanted to take the flag in order to keep the house alive. Which wouldn't work of course. The end happened. It was over. People go on with their lives and sometimes what they do next is even better. Or people forget. They allow themselves to be caught up in something and then they brush it off. The house was not the house anymore and it would never be again. I knew that but I had to do something. I had to *act*. I needed some sort of pure, driven cleansing to happen. I had to burn the flag. There was no other option.

For months after the party James and I had a vague sort of unrealized plan to steal the flag. We talked about it often but like most of our plans at the time it never got off the ground.

One night that summer, James, Tyler, Sadie, and I stayed up late drinking this big jug of Carlo Rossi Burgundy and listening to Hella's newest record over and over again (on both speeds, like Tyler loved). At some point, 4am, no, later, maybe 5, I knew it was time.

I got up off the couch and shushed the room. "Shh, okay, listen. Okay, guys. Let's go capture the goddamn fuckin' flag," I said

32

and then everyone was excited.

We trooped on down there, sticking to the alleyways and darker side streets, stopping to sit on curbs or garden walls and drink the last of the wine, all full of noble purpose and (what we thought was) righteousness. For Tyler and Sadie (and maybe even James) it was more a fun crazy thing to do. I wanted them to feel like I did, but I knew they didn't. Still they were caught up in the moment and I let myself imagine that they felt it just as much as I did. I needed to believe we were all doing this for the same reason. Even if they were faking it a little it felt good to be together. It scared the hell out of me to think James, of all people, didn't feel this as much as I did. Knowing (I would later find out) that he didn't care as deeply as me, that he didn't have the same ideals was heartbreaking. We're not together anymore but we're still friends. I wish he was more like me but maybe he's happier because he's not. I'll give him that. I can understand wanting some distance from the shitty evilness of the world. I don't know, maybe I wish I was more like him. Back then I lived for parties and believed in having fun above all. I still do but my work keeps me away from enjoying myself a lot of the time. James has always been optimistic and he lets things slide off his back. (I've been that way before but I'm not that way now.)

Anyway, we took our time. Talking a lot. Saying big things and letting the grandness of what we were about to do color our speech with bold, wild ideas and words that would sound preposterous the next morning.

James (who was happy-drunk) kept saying, "I feel like *Robin Hood*," and I did too. We had a purpose. We were going to strike back for the neighborhood and the scene and win one for the good guys.

So we got to the house and there were cops everywhere. The place was a mess, a firetruck, an ambulance, squad cards with lights spinning and flashing on the line of houses and parked cars.

"What?" said Sadie. She just kept saying it over and over again. "What? What? What?"

33

A couple EMTs were on the lawn working on this older woman in a torn-open pink bathrobe. Full-on CPR, then the paddles, which was a horrible thing to see. The paddles pushed down, the body flopped up, then the paddles again.

We just stood there and watched them try to bring this poor fucking woman back to life and we stood there and we stood there and we stood there and they weren't having any success and by then Tyler and Sadie and I were crying and, argh, I hoped to god they'd save her.

Nothing happened. They kept working. We turned around and walked home.

The sun was beginning to come up over the housetops to the east and the four of us walked together and no one said a thing. It was a death toll ringing. The final toll. Not just for the woman (I hope she lived, I never found out) but for this thing I wanted so badly to be a greater part of my life.

We never went back.

TYLER:

It was good to hang out with kids like Frankie and James because that was really not me. I wasn't searching for myself like they were and I didn't need the same things they needed. I've always had a plan and these days I'm exactly where I hoped I would be. People change but I haven't changed much. The wild, manically-drinking, drug-guzzling Tyler Monahan isn't much different from Dr. Tyler Monahan, because I've always been on this path. Frankie and James, they were ... they are ... impulsive, naive, emotional. Everything they did they did last minute and reckless and most of the time what they tried to do didn't work. There was no premeditative thought. None at all. It was on the fly and unexamined and you've got to be very good or very lucky to succeed that way.

Frankie and James believed in things I enjoyed but didn't necessary have to have. They believed in the bands and they believed

34

in the scene. They believed in finding community and in people joining together in the name of something bigger than them. I was around for all that, especially the shows and parties, but really ... this sounds more dismissive than I'd like ... I was just blowing off steam.

Things like that party were fun but they were just parties. My prime directive was getting shit done. The rest was just ... the rest was all diversions, great, fun, thrilling diversions, but it wasn't all that important to me. You don't dwell on the past. You move forward, and if you do that and plan well and make calm, rational, deliberate choices along the way you'll find the present is a lot better than what came before. We all make mistakes and we all lose things but if you spend too much time looking back you'll never go anywhere.

The wild Tyler Monahan didn't exist on weekdays. I studied. I spent long hours in the chemistry lab and I tutored and I moved toward my goal at a nice, even keel. When I got there ... it happened faster than I thought ... I found I was happier than I imagined I would be. Or at least contented, secure in my place, if a little lonely because it was ... and still is ... something I did on my own.

Frankie and James have both had, well, to be honest, much harder lives than mine. I feel bad for them of course but we get what we work for and that's what they got. I'll always stand behind them and have their back. I mean ... this is serious: I'm *serious*, I'd give my life for those two and I say that without exaggeration but I know what I am and I know what they are and we're different animals.

I get sad thinking about them sometimes and when I do I feel old. I feel creaky and lonely and kind of ... kind of maybe cold? Yeah, cold. But then I remember the good things I have. The fact that we're only ... how would you say this ... only very ... tangentally involved in each other's lives these days is hard sometimes. We've talked about that, the three of us. Some fantasy part of me would love it if we all lived in the same house one day. We could grow old together, keep each other company. But I know it's just that, a fantasy. We're far too different ... now, just as it was back then.

35

Sometimes I think we truly are a lost generation. Not in the romantic, literary, Paris 1920s way Frankie always hoped but lost in the sense that America is this huge, vast, enormous place where everyone you know lives so astronomically far away from each other. There's a deep, sad estrangement in Americans. We're all so spread apart and isolated, living these remote, far-flung lives but we've chosen this. Maybe we could've chosen differently. I don't know. But this was what we wanted.

I'm not at all nostalgic for those days. I believe in living right now and being the best, happiest version of you that you can be, the past be damned. Just the same, I'd be lying if I didn't say the wild Tyler Monahan ... and he's still there ... wouldn't love to step back into the madness sometimes and feel all that ... all that energy bursting around him, *energy* that was not really his, but that he enjoyed nonetheless, and was caught up in, and if only for a short time, felt wholly, *substantially* alive.

JAMES:
The first few hours of the party were spent moving room to room watching whatever band was playing. At that point my bottle of MadDog was gone and I was floating along stupidly in a way I never would again, seeing the sights like an astronaut on a new planet or a tourist in my own neighborhood.

The later it got the more people arrived until you could barely get through the halls. At some point we ran into Ted Boone in a leather jacket and a very dirty Joy Division shirt who was visiting from Portland and dragged me, Tyler, and Frankie out behind the house and made us do shots of brandy with him while he told us about his plans to join the seminary.

"You guys, I'm doin' it. Next time you see me I'll be the Reverend Ted Boone." He made the sign of the cross in the air.

Tyler shook his head. "I don't believe that. You? There's no way. You *hate* Jesus."

36

"I think that's really sweet," said Frankie.

Ted Boone, smiled, pleased. "Yeah?"

"Yeah. I like that. It's sweet."

"You really believe in god?" I asked, handing the bottle back to him.

"Is that a trick question?"

"Because I'm *pretty* sure you've told me different, like, many, many times."

Tyler laughed and took the bottle from Ted Boone. "That bumper sticker on the old BooneMobile? The one that said 'Executing Jesus for Treason is the Reason for the Season.' I remember that."

Ted Boone laughed and shook his head. "I believe in whatever will get me where I want to go."

"That's kind of fucked-up," I said.

"James, Tyler, Frances, welcome to my world. Drink more brandy. You will start to believe in many things, great and small. Drink now because I am in a grand amorous mood and I must find sexual companionship of the young and firm-breasted kind or I will wither like the vine without shade."

"You're kind of a villain, Ted Boone. You know that right?"

"I *bank* on it," he said with an evil grin.

I took the bottle from Tyler and unscrewed the cap.

After that I was fucked. I lost Frankie and Tyler in the crowd and ended up alone in the house. I remember walking through the various rooms and it was like they were circus funhouse rooms, each its own realm. The rooms were packed so tight you'd have to climb over people to get to see the bands. Ratty punk kids with bullet belts and patched-up black denim. Older scene kids in perfect Levi's jackets and tight jeans and high-sole creepers. A famous artist from LA—very tall, vampiric in all black and sunglasses—in the corner talking to a couple girls and trying to play it low-key. Lots of cool Mexican goths with greased-up hair or Cleopatra eyeliner and a million tattoos. Lots of people were drunk. Lots of people making out. Upstairs there were

37

so many kids in the main room when the bands played the floor felt soft, like it was going to give way at any second.

The halls were just as crowded, people shoving to get through, kids writing on walls. Broken glass everywhere.

I remember Cedric and Omar from At the Drive-In playing some kind of deep, heavy, weird, improvisational dub under the name De Facto on the first floor. The room was very dark and people were jammed in like cigarettes in a pack, pressed up against each other, too close to move. Moving Units played downstairs too. It was dance music as punk and punk as dance music in the most spectacular way. The scuzziest of new wave, the catchiest too. You could tell they wanted to be there, wanted to be doing exactly what they were doing, and that was a fine thing to see. The Blood Brothers' set was manic and shaky. They were doing a lot of songs off *March on Electric Children* and they—the songs, I mean—were as frantic as they were heavy. It was so loud not all of it made sense but that was beside the point. It *felt* right, and anyway, disorder and correctness are not mutually exclusive like a lot of people will say.

FRANCES:
Seeing the Locust play was always pretty fuckin' amazing. Of all the bands in our scene their lyrics were the most political; they were anti-cop, anti-authoritarian. I don't think a lot of people got that at the time, because most of the bands in our scene weren't very political. In contrast to other scenes happening at the time, San Diego kids were more about pushing the boundaries of art and music and fashion, and that was good too.

Something I've learned these past few years is you need to have art with your activism and activism with your art. It's essential. If you don't find a little pleasure to offset the strain of fighting for a better world you burn out. These days most of my friends are either radicals or journalists who cover activist stories. They're believers. They're staunch and they get up every morning without much sleep and they do battle, but they're strained and ... they're *overwhelmed.* Almost across the board. You see it in their eyes. They're hurt. They're tired. I try to tell them we need to be more like the people our age from Paris in the 1920s, y'know, active, informed, but still down to party, still into art for enjoyment's sake. Sometimes they take my advice for a minute but it never sticks. I don't even take my advice most of the time. I know it would be healthy for me to slow down for a second and get drunk and go dancing or just chill the fuck out and read a novel or something but in the end the pull of my work makes recreation feel self-indulgent. I know how that sounds. I do. But, yeah, I don't like feeling frivolous, or that I'm wasting my time on things without meaning.

Looking back, I feel like that party was a thousand years in the past. The me that was there is the me that's here now but it's not been easy. I've been trying as hard as I can but some days I feel like a sinking ship. It's been a rough couple years.

JAMES:
After the bands played I wandered back to the front of the house— excited and in love with the world, in love with everyone I saw, and all the possibilities of being alive and willing to take risks and try bold things.

As I walked through the house alone I looked at everyone and I loved them all. Who were they? All those kids—drunk, sober, laughing, bickering, smoking, hooking up, arguing. I wanted to be everyone's friend all at once, to take each one aside and say, "Look, here we are; we're together for this one great thing. Why don't we all know each other? Who are we in this place and most of us strangers? I'm a nice person. Life is lonely. Let's be friends." My eyes were filled with tears. I was happy and drunk and I wanted so much.

Outside the house, kids were getting violent. Someone had pushed a couch off the second story balcony and somebody else tossed a handful of firecrackers into the yard and a few people got

39

hurt. I walked down the porch steps to see Frankie holding a white t-shirt to our sweet neighbor Jessica Colvin's face. She—Jessica—was sitting up against the white picket fence and blood was soaking through the shirt.

By then the cops had begun to arrive and they were out front questioning Omar and Cedric from De Facto next to their van and that seemed like the funniest thing in the world. I stood on the porch and snapped a picture with my disposable Kodak box camera. It felt like an important moment. Was it? Who knows what's important and what's not. At the time I thought to myself, "Things are happening right now and we're alive and the world is funny and okay and we can do whatever we want. The world that's happening now is a world we can change and control. We can make this world whatever we want it to be. We can rebuild the world in our image if we work together and we can crush the very foundations of the old order."

It's a good feeling to have that kind of confidence and optimism at least once in your life. I've had it since but never that idyllic, never that *sure*.

TYLER:
Fuck the police forever.

FRANCES:
What was it? Eight, ten squad cars? So many cops for just a house-party. It was asinine. We were having so much fun (dancing to the bands, going crazy in the pit, drinking wine, and everyone laughing, meeting new people, talking to strangers, cheering after each song like we were at a gladiator arena). As soon as the cops got there it was like a bucket of ice-water thrown in our faces.

JAMES:
Even those hundreds of billions of cops didn't bring me down. Maybe I was too drunk but I didn't feel at all bluesy until the walk home.

40

FRANCES:
The thing about James is he was always very hard to find after a party.

TYLER:
San Diego cops are the ugliest cops you'll ever see, which is funny because it's a city with a lot of attractive people. San Diego cops look like giant, dickish warthogs with mirrored sunglasses and mustaches. People call cops "pigs" but San Diego cops really do look like pigs. I used to have fantasies of just going out and killing a bunch of cops. Killing off the entire San Diego police force as a service to humanity. I mean of course I'd never do it but if I did I don't think I'd ever feel bad.

JAMES:
I might've puked on someone's mailbox half on purpose. No, totally on purpose. It was so gross. Funny though.

FRANCES:
After I found James and Tyler we stood on the sidewalk and James and I tried to talk Tyler into not driving home. We told him he always had a place on our couch and he told us he knew that and that it was something he knew he could always count on. But he left anyway. James hugged Tyler. I hugged Tyler. And he left. I was kind of mad to be honest.

TYLER:
Frankie called out to me as I was walking down the sidewalk and she was like, "Tyler! You're totally going home to study, aren't you? Admit it!" I turned around and shrugged and played it off but she was right. I had a test on Monday.

JAMES:
Tyler would always go home after parties or shows and study the

41

hardest fucking subjects no one else in the world understands.

TYLER:
Sometimes I would go home after a party and I'd be out of my head on speed or ecstasy (usually dropping Joey Carr off first who would be just as destroyed) and I'd go do my homework and listen to Debussy. Debussy and organic chemistry and cocaine. It was some surreal shit. The raven was right ... nevermore.

JAMES:
I remember driving around with Tyler and Joey Carr and both of them were doing lines at every stoplight like a couple idiots and Tyler had Wagner or some dumb bombastic crap blasting out of his speakers. It was horrible. I hated that shit. Those two were on a whole different wavelength.

TYLER:
After I said goodbye to James and Frankie I walked to my car and saw two people having sex in the backseat of a Jeep. You could see the soles of the girl's sneakers pressed up against the glass and the back of the guy lurching against her. The Jeep was rocking side to side.

Someone else walking down the sidewalk (there were a lot of us) said, "Yo, get a *room*, muhfuckers," and everyone laughed.

Driving home I was so drunk the lights of the SeaWorld tower were blurring like a 300-foot-tall flashlight on the skyline. I remember watching it move and thinking, "It's going to fall. It's going to fall and crush poor Shamu." It didn't.

JAMES:
I was very drunk when Frankie and I walked home. She had her arm around me and held me up and we didn't say much. There was a gravity to the silence. We were both mixed-up inside and it would be days before we talked about it.

FRANCES:

Years later, thinking back on it, the hardest thing for me was watching everyone leave. For a few hours it felt like we were all in this thing together, that there was some kind of greater commonality between us, but we left. We left in pairs or alone. We left drunk, high, sober, happy, sad, afraid, laughing, but we left.

While the cops were inside breaking up the party and Tyler was who knows where and James was up the block I remember standing on the porch alone with everyone coming out of the house behind me. Just filing right out of the place as they were told to. Where were they going? They were going home, to parties, to TJ, to sleep it off, to eat, to fuck each other, to get more beer.

I saw a very drunk Ted Boone staggering down E Street toward 24th, walking in the streetlight, all yellow-gold around him, then into the shadows below the trees. At some point he put his hands on the trunk of a tree and vomited for a very long time. After that he walked on, and at the end of the block (by then he was barely there in the fog) I saw him open the passenger-side backseat door of his car and climb in. It was the last time I saw him.

I watched a couple teenage boys walk past, holding hands, rubbing up against each other, pulling at each other's clothes, talking quietly. I'd seen them hook up earlier and now they were headed off to make-out or have sex. They were very much in love (or at least lust) and you could tell how much they wanted each other. It was sweet. I was envious.

Coming out of the house there were groups of drunken girls in fucked-up '80s cocaine businesswomen attire or stupidly tight, low-rise jeans and torn-up shirts, younger girls, older ones, but whoever they were they were together, a pack, a gang; they walked past me, groups of them, talking and laughing, and then they filed down the street to smoke on the sidewalk or piled into cars or kept walking until the fog swallowed them up.

Guys from the bands who played earlier walked past holding

43

guitar cases or carrying amps. A young girl with a Chelsea haircut (thick blonde bangs, a long strand down each cheek like sideburns, shaved in the back) walked down the steps with a huge watermelon in her arms.

I heard people talk as they walked past me. "Let's go get fucking burritos." "GoGoGo was sick, huh?" "Dude, fuck those wack-ass east county kids in the pit at Reagan Youth." "What time do you think La Posta closes?" "Did you really hook up with Susan Newell? You, sir, are a god." "I'm way too stoned for this many cops." "Geoff and Shanna totally made out in the alley. Finally, right?" "I have school tomorrow." "I'm so hungry I want to cry." "My feet hurt." "I hope we didn't get a ticket." "Taylor's band is hella lame but I'd totally bone him." "I have to call my mom." "Where did we even *park?*" "I'm as sleepy as a little baby frog." "My bike better still be there or I'll kill the world." "We should get pizza." "How much is a taxi?"

Watching them all leave was a heavy thing to see. It was an army retreating, leaving the front and going back to the world; already concerned with the next thing.

Where are they now? These days I don't see anyone from that time. Not even James unless he visits. A lot of them (most of them, I think) were sucked into the great pneumatic tube that takes you from your hopeful, idealistic youth into the dull drags of adulthood. They go mainstream, they have mainstream jobs, mainstream sex, mainstream relationships, mainstream families, mainstream tastes. Which isn't bad but it's not what I wanted back then, and it's not what I want now.

So they disappear. They drop out into a bland, safe, lifeless normalcy. Or they don't make it. Kids die. Or they burn-out. They stay in the scene but they stagnate and age badly and never make good on the promises of their youth. They waste the wonderful things inside them or they kill themselves or die of a fucking overdose like poor Marlon Garfield on the floor of a Burger King bathroom. When I do see someone from the past, someone who has let go of what they were, they look old. They look tired and swollen and bloated

44

like a blurry yearbook photo of themselves. All those fresh faces and confidence ... all those dreams—they failed, or stalled (or changed).

The ones that didn't change, the ones that stuck it out, have had it harder. They still have their ideals. They've kept touring and making records or writing books or going to shows but life isn't easy on those who resist letting it bend them. A lot of them are doing even better than back then. Those are the ones who look like warriors. Wounded a bit but still standing. Those who still burn inside like a nuclear goddamn blast and live for their dreams and feel it on a daily fucking basis. They may not look as fresh-faced but they look strong; they look savage and beautiful and pure and they shine with a different kind of light.

I still want to see a better world and I want to have that kind of community I thought I had in those days but (at least lately) life has shown me a lonelier road. I hope it's not like this forever because for now my ideals are just as strong but my hope is fading. Did I make the wrong choice? Am I making enough of a difference to warrant the strain I've placed on myself? Would my life have been better had I stuck it out in San Diego, found another job after the magazine went down, rolled with the punches, changed as life wanted me to change? Who would I be? *What* would I be?

Fall is here and today I'm taking the bus to pick my boys up from preschool. As soon as they're asleep tonight I'll get back to work. Right now I'm researching local factory farms with water pollution violations as possible sites for my partner's drone investigations. It doesn't pay but it's the right thing to do and I'll work on it until morning, setting everything else aside for it.

Sometimes it's like dropping stones into a deep well where you don't get the satisfaction of hearing them hit the water. Other days it's better but I would be lying if I said it hasn't been the former more than the latter for a while now. It can be thankless, and frustrating. Still I work. I fight. I believe. Like yesterday, and the day before, I'll sit and type at my laptop by the window while the boys sleep in their room, in

45

this big rented house that's not mine, in this city where I know no one, and when the dawn comes I'll stop, make more coffee, and start the day.

JAMES:
Things haven't changed much for me since then. Only thing is I hardly ever see Frankie and Tyler anymore. Sometimes on holidays. Birthdays. If one of us is passing through the other's city. I never thought life would turn out like this, which is not to say I'm upset. I miss them, every day I miss them, but I like how I'm living.

The life I have isn't easy—money's always a problem, and like the old song goes, "the future's got me worried/such awful thoughts"—but I'm doing exactly what I want to be doing and that makes me feel pretty okay. I mean, not okay in the fair to middling sense but okay as in secure and happy and excited about what I have going. I'm in love—it's new love, the kind of love that can make you feel like you're truly in the right place—and I'm doing exactly what I hoped I would be doing back in the days of the party. It's happening. Not exactly as I hoped it would happen—because the world is a different place—but it's happening nonetheless.

Still, there are things I miss. I miss the feeling of being in a room where everyone is losing their shit to a band that sounds like nothing else. What I remember most from that night was the upstairs room and how good the music felt. It was so loud you could barely hear it but you could FEEL it. You felt it in the center of your stomach and in your muscles and deep inside your chest. The pit was far too big for such a small room. So many people in that tiny space throwing themselves left and right, and in the middle of it all this little, pale, brown-haired girl caught up in all the crowd-crush, eyes-closed, blood smeared around her mouth and down her neck, screaming and punching and kicking like her life depended upon it. You knew there was something deeper going on. There was an important thing at the center of it all. She had some kind of horror in her and she was there

46

to force it out. She was there to *heal* but in a powerful and scary and violent kind of way. I'll never forget the way she moved through the room and how the room bent out of her way and moved around her.

Epilogue
Agnes

As bodies knocked against hers and people fell down and were pulled back up again, and as she was soaked in the sweat of everyone else and they in hers, Agnes shut her eyes and let the music hit her like holding your arm out a car window to feel the air push back.

She thought of the wind in her face on the rollercoaster and she thought of the time she rode on the back of Steven's motorcycle and he took her up into the hills above Old Town to see the Spanish Mission and she held onto him and felt the air as a physical thing—an angry force, a strong hand and a door slammed, a magnet's pull or a jet taking off or the churning swell of the sea.

Agnes was thrown to the side and held back up, shoved forward and stopped by the damp wall of a body.

Blind, she felt the music and the people around her as she was knocked this way and that, grabbed by the waist, elbowed in the lip.

Blood, she thought, as a wave of pain throbbed from her teeth to the back of her neck.

She could taste blood.

Then another elbow caught her in the stomach.

The wind knocked out of her, she punched back (sightless) and didn't connect and fell forward and was pulled into a standing position again and her eyes opened and she saw the dim lights of the room and the people moving around her and the band, vicious but elegant.

She raised her face to the ceiling and spit out blood and saw it break into a spray of droplets in the yellow light.

Agnes shut her eyes again and was thrown to one side,

then the other, and the world broke in on itself with a clap like two hands coming together, and she spun wild circles, kicking, punching, laughing—laughing as she cried for Michael the Bear, loyal and true and dignified, and for Steven, weak and mean in his uncle's store and for Big Marcos who didn't know what time weddings were and for her parents and everyone's parents and for everyone everywhere. The crowd pushed. Agnes pushed back.

51

THREE.ONE.G →

This book is a collaboration between Three One G and Pioneers Press. Formed in San Diego near the turn of the last century by Justin Pearson, Three One G has released records from bands such as Black Dice, Unbroken, Retox, Antioch Arrow, Swing Kids, Moving Units, and the Blood Brothers. Recent Three One G titles have included 7"s by Metz, Hot Nerds, Zeus, Planet B, a cassette EP from Into Violence, and a set of songs by Locust bandmates Pearson and Gabe Serbian for the Asia Argento film Incompressa. Pioneers Press was founded in 2012 by ex-San Diegan Jessie Duke. Recent titles from the press include books by Julia Eff, Olivier Matthon, Matt Gauck, Craig Kelly, and Trace Ramsey, as well as Adam Gnade's *The Do-It-Yourself Guide to Fighting the Big Motherfuckin' Sad*, which was Powell's Books #1 small press bestseller for 2013, 2014, and 2015. Duke is a recipient of a 2013 Rocket Grant from the Charlotte Street Foundation and the University of Kansas Spencer Museum of Art with funding from the Andy Warhol Foundation for the Visual Arts. This is the first collaboration between Three One G and Pioneers Press.

About the Author

Adam Gnade was born and raised in San Diego, California. He now lives and writes on a small homestead farm near the Missouri River. His books are *Hymn California* (DutchMoney, 2008), *California* (Double Suns, 2010), *The Do-It-Yourself Guide to Fighting the Big Motherfuckin' Sad* (Pioneers Press, 2013), and *Caveworld: A Novel* (Pioneers Press/Punch Drunk Press 2013). His next novel will be released in Summer 2016.